How to Be Alone

Also by HEATHER NOLAN

Land of the Rock: Talamh an Carraig (poetry)

This Is Agatha Falling (fiction)

HOW
TO
BE
ALONE

HEATHER NOLAN

Edited by Bethany Gibson.
Copy edited by John Sweet.
Cover and page design by Julie Scriver.
Cover image: Kelly Holt, *Streetstyle 23* (detail), 2022, 12.5 × 12.5 × 2.5 cm,
archival digital photo collage, acrylic paint and spray paint on Kozo paper
mounted on a birch panel. www.kellyholtart.com
Printed in Canada by Marquis.
10 9 8 7 6 5 4 3 2 1

Library and Archives Canada Cataloguing in Publication
Title: How to be alone / Heather Nolan.
Names: Nolan, Heather, 1992- author.
Description: Two novellas.
Identifiers: Canadiana (print) 20230227201 | Canadiana (ebook) 20230227260 |
ISBN 9781773102856 (softcover) | ISBN 9781773102863 (EPUB)
Classification: LCC PS8627.O586 H69 2023 | DDC C813/.6—dc23

Goose Lane Editions acknowledges the generous support of the
Government of Canada, the Canada Council for the Arts,
and the Government of New Brunswick.

Goose Lane Editions is located on the unceded territory of the Wəlastəkwiyik
whose ancestors along with the Mi'kmaq and Peskotomuhkati Nations signed
Peace and Friendship Treaties with the British Crown in the 1700s.

Goose Lane Editions
500 Beaverbrook Court, Suite 330
Fredericton, New Brunswick
CANADA E3B 5X4
gooselane.com

For Jessie

BOOK ONE

How to Be Alone on
Boulevard Saint-Laurent

ONE

I am walking up Boulevard Saint-Laurent in the gathering heat. In the window above the pawnshop opposite, a laptop propped on a TV stand plays a movie to no one. In the next window, lovers sit silent at a table. Battle stances.

...

As the first rumble snaps, we all drop the pretenses. Strangers in the square make eye contact. Was that thunder?

I stand very still and try to catch their eyes again, but our moment is over. I long for another crack.

...

The restaurant isn't the type I would ever go to. I mean, the uniform was fancier than anything I had ever worn and I was a dishwasher. Wool-blend trousers in all that putrid steam. I came into the job by fluke, some old roommate desperate to get a shift covered, and the chef was so mad at the roommate he gave me his job. I wouldn't have stayed on if it wasn't for Bea. She was one of those women who had a way of drawing people into whatever she did. I have spent my whole life following after those women. Wide-eyed, nodding dumb, heart thrumming in my chest.

...

Rule number one: don't join in on conversations between strangers on the bus.

...

I'm sitting on the edge of a fountain when three women stop to ask where the *musée* is. I mention about the humidity, tell them I heard thunder earlier. They nod slowly, ask if it is the long white building across Place des Arts. I tell them about the band I saw last night. They point out the big round building behind me. I wonder out loud if it would be weird to dip my toes in the fountain to cool off. Two of the women start to drift away. The third says, hey listen. Asks about the museum again.

I put my feet in the fountain. Tell her it's closed today.

...

I remember when I first met Bea. I had gone to some cocktail bar with all the servers. Hadn't realized when I tagged along that there was some kind of pecking order and I was at the bottom of it. They ignored me, ordered expensive drinks that came in tippy glasses. Talked over each other about some fancy wine crap I zoned out on. Dark fruits. Subtle hints. Tannins. Tannins. Tannins.

Bea was the one who broke through that. She came over and sat beside me. Asked me where I was from. Nodded like she was interested in the answer.

I guess that night was the first time Derrick offered me coke too though. You win some you lose some, right?

...

I am old enough now that I get stomach ulcers when I try to live off cigarettes and coffee and hard liquor like I did when I was younger. I stare moodily at kids who still can and I want to yell *eat some fucking fibre,* but that seems weird so I don't. I take frequent trips to the bathroom.

...

I keep repeating *il vaut mieux*. Or maybe *il sera mieux*. Stop switching to English, guys, I'm trying to live my delusions here. What will my therapist think of this? Only I don't have one yet, I'm on the wait-list because the government doesn't think I am a serious threat to myself.

...

Someone asked me for something recently, but I can't remember who it was or what they needed.

...

When a man texts me back, I get wary and I tell him I'm not looking for anything serious. I guess that's what my therapist would call a defence mechanism if I could fucking get a therapist.

...

I started trying to psychoanalyze myself in the meantime. Do you think this is a good strategy Y/N?

Should I go back to the restaurant and pretend I was just sick when I walked out in the middle of my shift six weeks ago Y/N?

Do I have stomach ulcers am I dying Y/N?

If I screen my calls and don't check the mail, does my credit card debt still exist Y/N?

Am I just dehydrated Y/N?

Wait, what's my stop Y/N?

Am I making everyone on this bus uncomfortable by humming Y/N?

...

Bea was the bartender at the restaurant and she wore a black dress that swished around her like vermouth when she moved. This one time the bar was short-staffed so they let me be her assistant and I mixed the simple syrup with the wrong ratio and she looked at me blankly and she said what the hell am I supposed to do with this and I felt like I was going to throw up.

I heard later that Derrick took her job. That makes me fucking sick.

...

Okay, so if it is weird to be alone all the time and weird to talk to strangers, like you see the problem here right?

...

Define "stranger."

...

Every time I see some old man with his shirt off in a parc, I want to take mine off too, but something tells me he would miss the point. They always miss the point.

...

This one time I found Bea smoking on the deck off the dining room at the end of the night with all the lights off, and she had just come back from visiting family in Scotland and she said, Well no, they aren't really my family. One of them sent me an email by mistake one time, the wrong Bea McIntyre, and I answered and we've been in touch ever since. I visit every year.

I just nodded along. Only Bea. That's the sort of thing Bea did.

...

Earlier I was drinking a bottle of wine on the sidewalk and this guy told me I was going to get a fine and I pretended I didn't speak French, but then I realized he had said it in English, so I walked a few blocks and drank the wine on that sidewalk.

I got a fine.

...

Do people still live in New York?

...

When the rain starts, it's like a pipe has burst in the sky and everyone scatters. I run for the gazebo up ahead in Parc Little Italy where a crowd has huddled together. I hover near the periphery and light a cigarette and a man on his phone says into the receiver, I think the weather is calling for rain, as he stares out into the deluge. I cackle at this. He looks up with a grin, but it falters and the chasm widens between me and everyone else. I walk back out into the rain.

...

That first night when I met Bea, me and her and Derrick wound up at Chez Dev where the windows were all blacked out, an ashtray on the table, the whole place a cloud of smoke. There was a portrait of Robert Johnson on the wall and his eyes were boring into mine and he leaned over and said, Let me tell you a little something about making a deal with the devil.

...

Every time I go on a date, I drink too much and start trying to scare them off by talking about drugs or my childhood. Works every time.

...

Can we confirm that childhood just fucks us all up why don't we just get rid of childhood?

...

Rule number two: a deal's a deal.

TWO

Do you ever think the hum of deeply engrossing conversations and chirping birds and laughing children is just some background track for a movie because the real world is actually a silent, morose tomb we all suffer in alone?

No? Okay. Whatever you say.

...

Wasps have been circling me all week. Fucking sting me already.

...

One night last year, me and Bea and Derrick stole a bottle of wine from the restaurant when we got off work and climbed the fire escape and sat on the roof and I kept staring at the way her fingertips traced her collarbone. Like she was checking to make sure it hadn't escaped her skin. I think I was kind of in love with her, but I wasn't out then.

...

That feeling when you sit on a bench in a parc but it's uncomfortable so you want to get up and go sit on the grass, but you don't want everyone in the whole parc to know you've got commitment issues.

...

Seriously though, if my body has the nuance to sweat when it gets overheated, you would think I could manage a basic human interaction.

...

I met this guy Sid one night at Chez Dev and we started sleeping together. We were out one night and one of his friends took out a baggie and offered a key to me and said, Ladies first and Sid literally stepped in front of me and said, Capital-N No she doesn't do that and I said, Want a fucking bet, and took three hits.

I've always had a problem not taking a challenge.

...

Do you think these wasps were sent from hell to punish me for using my roommate's hair conditioner?

...

The first woman says, Je crois qu'il m'aime.

The second woman says, Très utile.

The third woman says, Attention, code soixante sur la ligne orange.

...

Did I close my tab last night?

...

I went through this weird phase last spring when Bea wasn't around much. I slept with way older men and one of them still likes to text me jokes and weird facts and some of them are pretty good. But the other day he said he wanted to send me a sexy pic and I was drunk and a little uncomfortable but I didn't want to make him feel like an ass and I don't get many messages these days so I just said, Well, where is it then, and I guess that was a bit of a mixed message, you know? But he just sent the photo now, two days later, and it's of a woman sucking his dick and I can't put my finger on it but that feels a bit weird, so I guess I have to block his number too.

...

The sharp metallic sound of a spoon tapping the edge of a pot comes from a window above me. Two voices murmur in a sultry little debate about more oregano.

Nausea rips my body open like a zipper.

...

It never occurred to me that Derrick and Bea might have been sleeping together. I mean, it was a bar scene. Everyone slept with everyone. I guess it doesn't really matter either way.

...

Me and Bea were walking up Saint-Laurent a few months after Leonard Cohen died and she pointed out his house and said we should drink a bottle of wine in front of it and so we did, we just drank a bottle of rosé on a bench in Parc Portugal staring at the house, and I left a pack of Du Mauriers on the step when we left.

Okay it was one cigarette, but I think he would have appreciated the sentiment.

...

Am I hungry or is it the tumours/ulcers/etc.?

...

I guess that time on the roof with the collarbone there were things Bea said. She said it's nice to have these memories. Or it will be. There was a past-tense thing. I wonder if she knew then. I wonder if Derrick did.

...

When I woke up this morning, there were outbound calls on my phone to a bunch of people that it would be very inappropriate to booty-call.

Like one of them lives in Vancouver.

...

I had a dream that I was playing on a set of monkey bars and I fell straight down in the sand and broke my back and the restaurant manager came over and told me he was suing me for not washing plates counter-clockwise.

...

Remember that time when a dude texted me a photo of another woman sucking his dick?

...

Derrick had this nickname for us. The Three Devs. It was a joke, he said it the one time and we all laughed and that was it. Then months later he said it again in a pleading voice. But we're The Three Devs. I said I didn't want a drink and he said, But we're The Three.

I can't remember now who it was he was trying to convince.

...

The funny thing about Derrick is I don't remember a single real conversation. Come to think of it, I don't know if we ever really said much when Bea wasn't there with us. Mouths alternating between beer bottles and cigarettes. She was always the one who made the plans. She was always the one with something to say.

And here I am, the only one alone on Boulevard Saint-Laurent.

...

What the fuck does touch and go mean?

...

A tourist stops me to ask for a restaurant recommendation and I say, Idk dinner isn't really my thing I'm more of a drinks person. T'sais?

...

Is there anything worse than a restaurant full of people having a nice time?

...

It kills me that all my memories of Bea are with Derrick too, the three of us spent so much time together. We'd get off work at 3 a.m. and go to Chez Dev until 8, pass out for a few hours, and be back at work for noon. We spent every night together in that dingy bar and then Bea didn't come for a few weeks and when she came out again I kept buying her shots and finally she said, I'm not supposed to drink right now because I have cancer. Holy shit. She said, Honestly, it's no big deal, it's one of those easy ones, routine procedure. I had no idea she was lying.

I took the train to Kingston and found her grave. Long, low rattle of a single motion, letting my eyes slide out of focus through the river valley. It was the first time I'd left the island in years.

The grave was new; I had to search for hours through the little wooden placeholder crosses until I found the one with her name in faded Sharpie. Holy shit. How are you the one that's down there it should be me it should be me it should be me.

THREE

There's a festival on Avenue du Mont-Royal and everyone is just standing around staring at each other. The
music echoes off the Pharmaprix and people's sun-
glasses and the cans of beer in their pockets and the
cross on top of the mountain so it's hard to tell which
direction the stage is in. I guess it could just be a set
of speakers.

...

Bea hadn't told anyone else at the restaurant. Or at
least nobody talked about it. The day after she told me
and Derrick, the other bartender, Stan, was covering
her shift. I hovered around him shining martini
glasses until they were so clean the tense squeaking
echoed back to the kitchen and Chef came in and told
me to do my own damn job. Derrick was straightening
forks on tablecloths with his back turned. I glanced

back as I left the room, looking for the space she'd left, but it seemed like it had sealed behind her.

...

Restaurant work has a way of branding you. It has a way of sucking you down into the belly of the polished chrome kitchen, every surface shining violently so that you can't tell if you were the one who just ripped that line or if it was someone else entirely. It has a way of closing in around you so it's hard to remember what's happening outside.

...

So the real question is, Do I actually reek of cigarettes or is that just the inside of my nose?

...

Mostly the kind of people who came to the restaurant were just dull rich people. I didn't pay much attention to whose plate I scrubbed caked-on foie gras from. But one night some old rock star was in town and word reached the kitchen that he had fallen in love with Bea and asked her to dance right there in the middle of the bar.

Bea shrugged it off later when some other server showed me photos, but I stared. There she was, tossing the wild hair that she still had, laughing, looking at someone off to the left. The photo interrupted her eyes mid-sentence. I didn't even look to see who the celebrity was. Bea hadn't laughed like that in months.

...

I stop and open my phone and stare at her number and then put it away. An old habit I can't shake.

...

An old woman walking past just said, You will die when you are eighty-seven on a Thursday afternoon. I really hope she wasn't talking to me, that sounds like way too long.

...

And who was it that was standing just outside the frame?

...

I saw this girl Noémie one night at Chez Dev when Bea wasn't around. We'd met in passing, other nights at other bars. I tried to buy her a drink. She said, Oh no it's all right. I'll get one.

I said, No, but like can I buy you a drink? She said, Oh. Well I don't know. I mean I'm straight. But. Maybe.

...

Where is a good place to be surrounded by people but they all leave me alone?

...

I keep forgetting that Derrick was still with Kit then. They broke up around the time Bea started treatment. I forget they were still together because what I remember is the trio. But Kit came out for a drink sometimes. Other people from the restaurant did too.

I liked Kit. We drank a bottle of whiskey in the bathroom at Chez Dev once, sitting on the counter comparing the people we'd slept with in common. That was the sort of thing. I met her for a drink once, after they broke up. She took me to a poetry reading where they gave trigger warnings before poem after poem about assault. We were crammed in the back by the bar and there were so many heads between me and the door. So I just sat there against the cool, sharp edge of the stone bar, letting it jab into my spine with each poem.

After that I tried to tell her. Couldn't.

...

When I first moved to Montréal nobody I knew in the city answered my calls and for a few months the only person I talked to was the cashier at PA, so I bought groceries one yam at a time. My old roommate from Halifax used to call a lot back then. But now she won't talk to me and I can't remember why.

...

I'm sitting on a ledge by the stone archway in Parc des Amériques and a ringing fills the square. I look up to see a man in a suit standing in a row of BIXI bikes, flicking one of the bells with a concentrated look on his face. When he sees me watching, he just walks away. I can see his back retreating down Rachel for a long time.

...

Noémie took the drink. I put a hand on her waist. She whispered that she wanted to dance. Pressed herself up against me in the hazy bar. It wasn't the kind of place where people danced.

Something about that night has always sent my stomach rolling. Something about the way the roles shifted. My own body seemed to surge with a horrible power, gripping her hips and pulling them toward mine as she perched a cigarette between her lips and turned toward the bar. Hungry-looking men dove for their lighters. Three flames burst bright while a fourth shed sparks. Arms retreated, but only just. Is that the way straight men act? Trying to capture coyness in a clenched fist?

Or was it just that I kept imagining she looked like Bea when she turned away and all I could see was her long dark hair?

...

Bea was distant then. We tried to call. We did. She would just say she was too tired today. Tomorrow. Next week. It's no big deal, she said.

Me and Derrick went to Chez Dev. We waited for her there. That's what we did.

...

Seriously, why am I having heart palpitations just stop?

...

I've been noticing that I keep tabs on different possible ways to die at any given time. When I walk into a building, I look to see if there are any good balconies or an elevator shaft. Not that I intend to use them or anything, but I do like to know what my options are.

...

Should I pick up some wine and drink it in that parc up ahead Y/N?

...

In the morning Noémie put her clothes on and said, Yeah I'm straight. We slept together for a few weeks after that until some guy Adam threatened me for obstructing his dating prospects or something. I mean, I don't think he threatened anything specific. But there was the threat.

...

So you know the metro smell, right? What the fuck even is that smell like what am I smelling?

...

We are all going to pretend my skirt didn't just blow up, right?

...

Bea came out one night and Noémie was sitting at the bar when we got to Chez Dev. I did a significant eyeball thing at Derrick and he got the first round while me and Bea went to get a table. I insisted on one in the back corner instead of our usual.

Noémie followed Derrick back anyways, swaying a little. The three of us sat there not looking at her.

Eventually she just wandered off to flirt with someone at another table, returning only to ask if she could sleep at my place. I looked up at Bea. She shook her head. I shook my head. When Noémie left again, Bea leaned over and said, You can't let people use you like that.

I spent the rest of the night folding the soggy label of my beer into tiny pieces.

...

I met Derrick way before the restaurant. We worked together at a coffee shop in Saint-Henri when I first moved to town. I remember his first shift. He showed up with a cigarette tucked behind his ear, clutching a worn Walt Whitman book. He seemed like a good guy. Or anyways like the kind of person I would call a good guy in those days.

...

Do you ever think that trying to get through life without a cocaine addiction or getting assaulted is like trying to run a marathon in the desert or something where most people fall down?

...

That time at the bar where Derrick said to this other guy, like, Damn that's a fine piece of meat, or something gross like that and I really thought he was kidding and I said, You are so vile, and he said, I'd like to give that a go or something, and I just didn't take it seriously and he was a philosophy or poetry major so it seemed out of character but really there were so many warning signs and it was just inconvenient to pay attention to them.

Rule number three: there are so many signs.

FOUR

All week wasps have been hovering around me whenever I eat anything so I stopped eating and this
morning one stung me through my sandal as I was
walking to the metro just walking and honestly I can
hardly feel the swollen mass of pounding red flesh
burning against the leather straps I am so relieved to
have it over with.

...

All I kept thinking was, When will she lose her hair?
She'll lose her hair, won't she?

...

Here's the weird part. So there was this dude I met
after what happened to me who was an actor and he
was interesting enough but he looked just like Derrick
and the first time I saw him at a café I dropped my

coffee all over myself before I realized it was someone else, but now I am fixated on this other guy and I really want to fuck him. That's weird, right?

...

NTS: tell future therapist about this.

...

Self-diagnosis: maybe I am trying to take control of my past or something.

...

And then Bea was back. One day I showed up for work and she was there in her swishy dress, and she moved a little slower and her skin looked tight on her face, but she was back, and when I hugged her my face was engulfed in that wild hair (still there, still there) and I let it be and she said, It's okay. I said, I tried to call and she said, I know you did. Then Derrick showed up and he said, Let's get together after work. I was relieved he'd said it first.

...

This searing pain in my head: Tumours or too many cigs or didn't brush my teeth for a few days?

...

Bea came out to the bar. She just sipped water, but there we were. Sitting around a table at Chez Dev. Derrick ripped celebratory lines and I tried to fill her in on what she'd missed. I couldn't think of much to tell. Derrick had this weird cheery tone. Bea just smiled, she just said, It's good to be back. Derrick said, It's like nothing ever happened.

After a while I started following him to the bathroom to get a bump too. At some point I noticed Bea had a whiskey in her hand.

...

Burnt hair and ammonia knock me off balance when a salon door blows open. Long dark hair. Wild mass of it like an animal. When. When did she lose it. Where did it go. What happened then.

Ferme-là, someone is shouting. Les guêpes!

I don't realize I am running until I reach the wall of traffic at St-Joseph and have to stop and wait. My legs argue that this is just the opportunity I've been waiting for.

...

I was surprised to see Bea at work the day after her reappearance at Chez Dev. I hung close before service started, brought her coffee and water. Saved an extra staff meal for her. She looked into the bowl of goulash. Thanked me so sincerely I felt it in my pelvic bone. Later I heard her tell another server that she was on a special diet or something as she tipped the gluey clots of cold pasta and cheese into the garbage.

After service I sprinted up the stairs still soaked with sweat and greasy dishwater, ran into the bar. The other bartender Stan gave me a disgusted look. She's gone home to rest, he said.

...

I've been waiting at this light for fifteen minutes and the crosswalk sign hasn't come up. Should I push the button again or just take a different street?

...

Bea was at work all that week. Except she was always gone by the time I got off. Didn't answer her phone. By the next week she had stopped coming in again.

...

The last time the three of us went to Chez Dev it didn't last long. I don't remember much. What I know is that we had just sat down and Bea was ordering a drink and Derrick was saying yes. Excellent. Just like old times. And my first beer went down quick and when I started my second something happened. I was sitting there looking at Bea in the yellowy glow of the lamps thinking she looked healthier, less pale, and then parts of her started to disappear like burnt film. And I said, Shit guys. Fuck. Make sure I get home.

That was the last time I ever saw her. Letting a slant of light persuade me she was going to get better, as some drug obliterated the whole image.

...

I'm drinking a cheap bottle of dep rosé on a bench in the dark and I hear voices up ahead. The guy at the crosswalk is yelling, It's going to be good you're going to be fine, after the girl.

I consider calling out, You can't possibly know that, but I can't afford another public intoxication fine.

...

I can't decide if this balcony is high enough to jump off, but the library in the Vieux-Port has really high lookouts over the reading room that could be good or like falling off a bridge over the river could work.

I'm fine.

...

I was sick for days after blacking out. Not sick exactly, but a little off. The next thing I saw after Bea's face was the ceiling of my bedroom sometime the next evening. Only it wasn't the ceiling I was focusing on, but the dust between my body and it. I moved like a slug toward the side of the bed and hurled all over the floor. Called in sick to the restaurant. Six hours after my shift had started. The dizziness lasted longer.

...

Lately I've had the urge to get naked a lot like not in a sexual way but in an animal way or a power way. Is that bad?

...

It was during the weeks after getting drugged that I realized how hard it is to stay away from a place like Chez Dev. I mean I was woozy and my stomach was clawing its way out of my body and I went back to work and I couldn't get away from Derrick. I said, Where is Bea? and he said, She didn't come in. But she'll be at Chez Dev. He followed me to the wine cooler, yelled through the frosted leaves etched into the glass door. You have to come. We're The Three.

...

Should I go to AA Y/N?

Serious question: Do you have to stop drinking to go to AA?

...

Okay so what if the poison from that wasp sting has reached my bloodstream? Am I dying?

...

Derrick just texted me and said, Hey can we go for a drink, I heard a rumour that I want to sort out with you.

...

Ha ha.

FIVE

I finish my cigarette and wonder what to do with the butt. I don't want to litter, or at least to look as if I litter, but there are no trash cans nearby so I put it in my pocket and keep putting my hand there to see if it is getting warm. I worry about catching on fire.

...

A strange feeling was all I had. I kept avoiding Derrick. I stopped texting Bea. One of the servers, Lesley, who I hadn't really noticed before, shared her sludgy green smoothie with me one day. It tasted like grass and dirt and whatever lies below that. She said there was some kind of voodoo aura thing surrounding me.

Yes, I said. Voodoo aura. How do I. You know. Exorcise it or whatever.

She looked at me with a concerned voodoo aura look.
Have you tried sobriety.

...

Things at the restaurant began to rearrange themselves. More and more it was Derrick taking Bea's
bartending shifts, not just whichever server they
could get. More and more he didn't ask why I wasn't
going along to Chez Dev. Didn't look me in the eye.

I started anticipating seeing Lesley at work, asking
her questions about the aura thing. The sommelier
cornered me and asked why I hadn't been cleaning
the wine bottles out. I hadn't realized anyone noticed
I usually drank the dregs at the end of the night.
Now there was the problem of the fruit flies. And the
cold waves of wooziness that kept coming. Washing
up over the sedimentary mess my flesh was starting
to feel like. Muscles clenched so tight, my whole
body seemed to contract into something smaller.
Something different.

...

I don't know why nobody brought Bea up in those
days. We all seemed to cling to the idea that she
was getting better, doing other things, and that was

all there was to it. Or maybe they all talked about it. Nobody talked to me anymore.

And then once I had quit the restaurant I couldn't face seeing her without somehow feeling like Derrick was there too. I didn't even know she had gone into remission until I saw the obituary.

...

It was when I heard of Kit's engagement to some guy she'd met in Toronto that I found Derrick again. Not that he'd gone anywhere. I'd been making excuses, avoiding going to the bar with him for weeks, and he had a new one now. I waited for him after work by the dumpster entrance, the usual, and he didn't say anything. But he'd brought the other bartender, Stan. And they let me follow along like a dog desperate for forgiveness. Or exorcism. To some cocktail bar with purple glitter reflecting off everything. I missed the dark, velvety haze of Chez Dev but I stayed and the girl who was hooking up with Stan joined and we drank. Just the one, I thought. Blend in. But I sipped steady, leaning out of the light, waiting for the right time to bring Kit up. We all went back to Derrick's. Sat around the table. He laid out a spread of wine and blow.

I just sat there and drank. Patient. Or that's what I told myself.

The other two eventually wandered off and Derrick turned to face me at that table and topped up my wine and took a line and I said, Look. I heard. You know. How are you?

Derrick's skin turned into stone, granite or something impenetrable, and he took out a key and shoved more up without even laying it out. Poured more wine into my cup so it pooled out onto the table.

Whatever, he said.

Fuck her, he said.

I don't think you mean that, I said.

No, I wanted to fuck her, he said, throwing a gesture toward the door Stan and the girl had left through.

But how do you feel? I said.

Fuck off, he said.

I drank quietly awhile and I think he tipped the bottle more and more and I said, Have you heard from Bea?

and he shrugged and I said, I should go. He said, No. I got to my feet and it didn't work and they weren't quite under me and I hadn't had a drink in weeks now, not since the blackout not since. How much wine. Did he. Was it.

I said, I might just lie down a minute. I tripped toward the couch.

Then he was dragging me toward his bed by the fucking collar.

...

Is it weird that I just want to make eye contact with strangers Y/N?

...

Two days after that I was scheduled to work with Derrick again and I couldn't get my shift covered and I guess I hadn't processed it yet anyways and every time I saw him all night I would just drop whatever I was holding. That night I broke twenty-one wineglasses, thirteen water glasses, three plates, and a jug. Eventually the manager sent me home early.

...

Actually what happened was I told the manager everything and asked if I could move my shifts around and he said we all have to make sacrifices.

...

When the obituary popped up online I said, No. No, it has to be the other Bea McIntyre. The one from Scotland. I texted her. I didn't call. I texted her and I said, Bea. Your friend. Your cousin. I said, Bea I'm so sorry. Give me a chance. I will be better.

Obviously, there was no answer.

...

The ding my phone makes for a new message is so foreign now I don't react at first. When I do open it, I see it's a text from Lesley. Come over, she says. We'll toast.

We sit around the room staring in different directions, seeing nothing. Then someone says something, remember that time. And we all open our jaws and pull laughter from some cold, clenched muscle in thin threads. I keep checking over my shoulder but there is no sign of Derrick.

I don't know anyone here, not really, just their faces. I go for a smoke and it's a cold night, unseasonable, the first thing of winter, and Lesley comes and stands and breathes out of the far side of her mouth and she doesn't say, Where have you been? so I do, I say, Where was I? And Lesley says, It's okay.

A sharp pain stabs my temple and I wince and I say, Sorry, all these weird pains since the time I stopped drinking. I take a sip. A gulp, really. And she says, No, wait, let yourself feel it.

And we go back in and sit there together not saying anything, but sitting there together. And it isn't as bad as being alone.

...

I'm sorry, I whispered into the dirt.

I know, I think she would have whispered back, but you're a dork for buying flowers.

...

I usually manage to skirt around losing control, but I guess that just depends who you ask.

INTERLUDE

INTERLUDE

Light. Flash. Light. Slide. Light.

Little square. Little rectangle.

Slide past. Slide past.

Slow.

And there's the voice and the door and the hydraulics and we are picking up speed.

We sway together we sway at sudden turns or the quick melody of opening doors we move we are an orchestra we are a symphony we are a ballet we are a collective noise project we are a hundred rumbling microwaves we lean like acrobats when the train takes a turn.

Each stop is a journey a trip a vacation an artist residency a year abroad. There are too many narratives down here they all cross and blend they collaborate on uncertain terms and leave one party with all the royalties and the other puts down their briefcase and climbs up the windows and howls through the long dark tunnels.

Nobody gets off we are all going out to Honoré-Beaugrand and then we'll break free of these tracks we'll go to Rimouski we'll go to Labrador. We'll burrow like worms through the earth we are worms now we are losing our bones. If you cut off my arms I will grow new ones right from the bloodied stumps.

I want to say something here now in this tunnel rocket under downtown. I want to say we're here together I want to say it is us and our lack of bones and I want to say we're going places and I want to say it all I want to talk to a stranger I want to be charming and not disturbing I want to say I won't cut your arms off even if they will grow back.

Now we stand shoulder to shoulder face to armpit backpack to eye socket crowd in clusters around the metal things to hold and others just stand there, packed in close enough to be braced.

I lean in.

A shoulder on my arm.

An elbow in my waist.

Close my eyes and sway.

Feel the jostle. Look to see what they are reading.

Can a body communicate like this?

Is this enough?

But there is a man back there.

Then it's fast and the people bodies pushing.

I am a cave a cavern I hollow out to keep my shoulders from touching but there it is it is it is.

Long high frequency as someone grazes my arm and I step back into the soft wall of another body and we're all sweaty palms and backpacks and the rattle rattle roll and we brace against nothing bracc against body to body to body and we go farther underground.

Sudden slow.

Lose my balance.

Face first.

Backpack armpit metal pole.

Suspicious eyes.

Red light coming now tiles long lane Expo orange curved lines McGill.

Bodies packed on the platform some push out some push in I shuffle I shuffle back behind the pole I'm in an armpit again.

We go down dark.

Downtown they all have cases to carry nobody speaks.

Cling to this pole slick with whatever is on their hands our hands we jostle around like kids at a maypole there is an intimacy. Is that wrong to say?

Is it wrong to consider this an intimacy?
Newspaper pages gather around our ring of feet I
feel I am being planted.
Ring around the rosie.

There's a man back there who looks like someone.
There's a man back there who looks like someone.
There's a man.
This time I look he is just another body.
This time I look he is someone.
Try to see his hands.
Someone blocks the way.

Pointing down picking up speed all those social
arrangements let slack.
In the dark underground we dance throw ourselves
at the windows feast on the contents of shopping
bags, sacrifices of bank documents and uniforms cry
out cry out cry out all the pain in those expensive
buildings above us, but we'll stand numb at our metal
poles by the next stop and the people press in.
Each stop we are a little more wild-looking.

Down and down and a light and the dark and a light.
Things flash no they don't I flash we flash.
Under the city under the city.

I look back and he could be someone.

He could be.

The doors try to close we are packed too tightly in they won't close.

Little woman cold techy voice little woman is angry.

How hard to be trapped.

Half in half out.

How long would you last?

Nice haircut be careful be careful the eyes it's in the eyes make sure you check them what do you see there.

Get the photos developed look for the eyes but they burned like acid through little holes little holes doesn't that tell you.

What's that in his pocket?

And he has done his little magic trick he combed his hair and now the eyes are on me he quoted Simone de Beauvoir and he read everyone a poem and it's my fault.

His magic trick.

High-frequency whine shimmer metal metal metal.

Thousands of tons of dirt and concrete and bones and cracked old foundations.

Everything the city ever tried to be.

The weight of all that.

I lean back against the door to free myself from the tangle of limbs grasping out for something to hold on to.

I don't want to hold on.

Is it him?

Arpeggios of machinery down down underground down down the weight pushes.

He is looking at me.

He is looking at me.

I can't move. Wedged into this space this door and the little woman will be angry and there is no path for my body there are other bodies and he is standing up.

The train is moving so fast we can't feel it but for the little jostle and the people pressing in and in and in and nobody gets off the train they just get on and on and the bodies come closer.

I shift my weight I try to indicate I point to the other end of the compartment I want to edge away I want to move and the person in the way just shrugs just gestures around with their hand to say what can I do what can you do. We are here now. We are on this train ride like it or not and I do not. But I agree that we are here now.

The man looks like someone and he has stood up from his seat. He is holding the top rail he is moving through as though there are not bodies everywhere he is looking at me.

And these people these bodies they let him pass they comment on his clean coat. He has carried a book and they like him they look at me now too these people these bodies.

They are looking at me.

Their eyes too are burning.

Walls close, little tunnel.

The man is getting closer the man is moving it is slow but he is moving and it is so slow it feels fast in this little rocket.

We glide we slide we rattle we are in a train car it is under the city we speed on and the time in these compartments is wrong is slower is faster it depends what direction we are moving and the people in their bodies have cleared they have made the space how have they made the space the man is walking now he holds nothing he is walking gracefully he is getting closer the people the bodies they block my way I am climbing I am stepping high over knees and the people make noises like bulls I am slipping between the bellies and the backpacks around the stroller under the shopping bags over the kids I am climbing I am climbing they are pulling at my ankles they want to drag me down I am almost through to the ceiling I am almost in the dirt I want to be higher than this underground tunnel I will be trapped in the subterranean and I look back.

And he is coming he is coming he is coming he will be coming my whole life.

BOOK TWO

How to Be Alone on
Rue Sainte-Catherine

BOOK TWO

How to Be Alone on
Rue Sainte-Catherine

ONE

Chloé was at the bottom of the twisted iron staircase. I was at the top. The stubbornness of a long, straight box had never occurred to me before now. I was guiding it toward the door of my new second-floor apartment. Chloé was bearing the brunt. We both knew this.

I bought everything from IKEA so I could make sure it got in through the narrow old doorway. I had never ordered furniture before. Shouldn't these companies at least tell you the dimensions of the package?

Mother had offered me her furniture. She had offered to buy me new furniture. She had offered to get furniture delivered and set up. She had offered to find me a nicer apartment. In a. Better. Neighbourhood. She had refused to set foot in this one. She had not left Westmount at all. She said, I don't get it. She buzzed around me, clutching at her own hands as I packed a single backpack and took the metro across Montréal to the Village.

I bought everything from IKEA so I could build something for myself. After Chloé ran off for work, I stood there surrounded by the pieces of my new life, but I couldn't seem to find the energy to open the boxes. I slept on the floor.

...

My apartment was just off Sainte-Catherine, farther east from the shining glass malls downtown.

A curtain of streamers stretched above the street in a long, languid rainbow. Looking up at it, I felt a surge of heat fill my chest cavity, as it often does when I am struck by beauty. The late summer sun shone through the streamers and I spun slowly on the spot, light winking through the colours.

Watch where you're going, dreamer boy.

I stumbled back to eye level, three men in short shorts smirking as they skirted me and drifted on.

I glanced up once more at the rainbow. I thought of Mother. I ducked into a Second Cup.

...

Classes didn't start for another week. I was transferring from McGill to l'Université du Québec à Montréal for the final year of my undergrad. I took to wandering the streets of the neighbourhood as though I'd never been here before. In some ways I hadn't.

...

I was sitting on a bench under the colourful canopy, an open book in my hand, my face pointed toward it. I wasn't reading. The sizzle of a saw touching a wooden board, entering it like butter, was so close it felt as though it was entering me. Farther down than my chest cavity. The man operating the saw across the street had taken his shirt off. His skin glistened. The other people working on the shopfront stomped around, called to each other, made noise with hammers and drills. Noise. I peeked at the man with the saw. Closed my eyes and waited for the saw to cut me open, let something out.

...

Mother was picking me up outside the cinema after a birthday party, getting out of the car to coo at the kids in my class. I was twelve, shivering near the car, watching her mingle and try to wave me over.

Levi, did you know Jeremy was taking drawing lessons? Levi?

Hollowing out my shoulders as if I could fold myself in half and disappear.

...

Chloé stopped by. The place looks great, she said.

Four days in and the only thing I had built was a nest of blankets on the floor in the corner. A few boxes had been opened, and small planks of wood lay scattered among instruction sheets and piles of tiny, delicate screws.

She took charge, like she always did. We'll start with the bed, she said.

I considered stopping her.

...

I met Chloé in first year, when we did a philosophy project together. I'd been slow to meet people, feeling like a loose feather adrift among the group activities that seemed to blossom all over campus. Chloé was everywhere. Every time I walked up the long path from Sherbrooke, there she was on the lawn with a megaphone or passing out flyers.

When our professor told us to choose a partner for our presentations, my skin pricked with sweat.

But Chloé turned around in her seat and said, All right, you're with me.

...

Chloé's voice came through my phone. You live closer than me now. You know where it is, ouais?

I said, Yeah, but I want to see you.

I stood on the sidewalk waiting for her, alert. People moved past as though trudging through deep mud. A sigh, a laboured breath, a sort of low hum that held the inflection of language. Then a sharp, The fuck you lookin' at.

I stepped back.

I couldn't tell who it was who had spoken. Ceaseless motion.

Chloé appeared, swung the door open. This was her domain, this sort of place. This vintage shop where people were dressed in quirky outfits and the shopkeeper handed us tiny glass bowls of Moroccan tea. Chloé said Salut to everyone and weaved her way around the store like her body did not understand the concept of hesitation.

She handed me gaudy eighties sweaters to try on, all neon shades of pink and seafoam green. The sight of them made me a little queasy.

What? she said. You're not in Westmount anymore.

I drifted off, let her statement echo through my body. Something about it felt discordant.

I bought a pair of black velvet loafers whose edges cut a line nearly to my toes. They bored Chloé, but I couldn't take my eyes off my feet as we walked back out onto the sidewalk. The tenderness of the tendons beneath my soft skin wrapped in velvet.

In the next shop I bought a linen shirt, opened the buttons halfway down. Stared into the mirror at my sternum, the bone pulling at my skin so I could see the ridges holding me together.

...

I went back to my small apartment, poured an IKEA wineglass full of rosé. I glanced out at the balcony, the afternoon sun through the leaves above at play. I stood next to the door. I looked out. Nobody was watching.

The rosé on my tongue was like a language I didn't understand but felt the warmth of. A Romance language. Italian. Sweet with a playful nip. On the second glass I swayed around my space, dancing to nothing but the ray of sun on the floorboards, the delicate, tangy pink I wanted to bathe in, the silence gathering and flowing around me like silk. On the second bottle I decided that rosé would be my signature drink. I opened my laptop and ordered twenties-style champagne coupes.

Mother called, asked me what on earth I was doing using my credit card to order tacky barware, was I free to come by and pick out some of the family crystal to use instead and what was she to think of my horrible little apartment and terrible choices and had I met any girls yet and maybe I should reconsider transferring because McGill had a much better reputation and why did I insist on studying in French and didn't I know that would limit me. I laughed at this, at which she begged my pardon and I came to and realized I wasn't listening to a voicemail but my actual mother demanding actual responses and I rubbed my T-shirt against my phone and shouted, Mother, can you hear me? I'm losing you? Bad connection? Mother? Hello?

...

I sat by the window drinking steadily and watching the world beyond the glass as the light leaned over and eventually toppled into a pool of indigo. Nobody was watching.

TWO

I sat in my favourite chair, the mod sixties faux leather one that bit my ass when I leaned to one side or the other, and I imagined I looked unreal. Not like the mythical or the imagined, but something less than real.

My apartment held the fragility of newness: furniture so cheap and stiff that everything still felt like cardboard, unused dishes smelling of vinegar and plastic, couch rigid with lack of familiarity with the human form.

For a moment I felt like I was lounging in an IKEA showroom. For a moment I felt like I did not exist at all.

I spun my chair around so as not to face the unease of the room, but to gaze instead out the window, down onto the ever-changing story that is Rue Sainte-Catherine.

...

When I was still living at home, Chloé and her partner Melissa often let me crash on their couch after a night out. Whenever I was too drunk to go home to Mother and her fuss. I had longed then for my own apartment, like Chloé, though she lived with five others, and Melissa had moved in before third year. They had things of their own, mostly picked up in thrift stores or alleyways, or even dumpsters, like the worn oak rocking chair in the living room.

I don't know what stopped me from leaving home sooner.

...

Chloé taught me French, or I picked it up from her. Sometimes I felt like it was a secret language of ours.

...

Mother never understood why I wanted to study in French.

But we speak English, she said.

Tu se dire comme c'nest pas la faute de nous-mêmes.

Don't start with that, she said. You know I don't understand.

...

I stood at the window with another glass of wine and I ached for classes to begin so I could meet people. It seemed the only way to do so was to participate.

...

Chloé came with me to check out UQAM. I met her by the Grande Bibliothèque, where she had been researching. She was always researching, ever since her and Melissa had split at the beginning of the summer. Divorced, she called it.

The campus looked more like an assortment of office buildings than a university, scattered across several blocks of downtown at the edge of the Village. At first this had appealed to me. Something different. But now, in the concrete heat, the campus seemed to lack something vital. I thought of the grand lawn that led into the McGill campus, the proud oaks, the classic brick buildings with the mountain rising behind.

Beauty, I said. Chloé looked up from her phone with a blank face, a face that had just re-entered the present.

Hm, she said.

That is what this campus lacks. Beauty.

Chloé smiled.

She said, I was texting a friend who goes here to show us around a bit. I squirmed. N'inquiète pas, she added, he's straight.

I looked at Chloé, said nothing.

As it turned out, her friend was a sculpture student and he took my request for beauty very seriously. He weaved through the long shadows of the city blocks as the sun glinted on buildings' glassy peaks. Through long corridors to a quiet library, all serious mahogany and leather, lit by glowing lamps. On again to tree-lined courtyards. I drank these visuals like coffee: sweet, thick nectar that sent tremors toward my fingers.

Chloé and her friend walked ahead as I filled my eyes.
Until I heard her ask about the queer scene. Clubs.
Societies.

I stopped walking. Neither of them noticed. The
colours drained like a bleach bath and I turned and
walked the other way.

...

Mother had loved to sign me up for things. Tennis
lessons. Model UN. The volunteer list for some city
council campaign. This past spring she'd even signed
my name to a petition supporting the banning of
religious symbols.

Staring at the thin gold cross resting on her white
clavicle, protests arranged themselves in my mind.
But as ever, I froze. I didn't know how to reverse what
she'd done. The only thing that seemed logical to me
was to take my name away from her. Get as far away
as possible.

...

As I walked home from campus, I began to consider
the idea that maybe I didn't want to be seen at all.

Maybe being alone wasn't some failure of human function, but a haven all its own. A freedom.

...

I remember, vaguely, how my mother was when my father still lived in Montréal. I don't remember a time when I wasn't aware of his affair, though Mother said nothing about it. It is her that I remember most from those years. When he came home from one of his long trips, took up his space at the head of the table, she tied an apron around her dress and poured cup after cup of tea with a manic grin on her face. After he was gone again, it always took her some time to find her way back.

I once caught sight of her, crying, through an open doorway as he drove away. She looked like she was deflating.

...

The only family I'd ever felt any real connection with was my uncle Robbie. He was Mother's brother and nothing like her. I mostly remember him being around when my father wasn't. My father ignored my mother completely, but his eyes followed Robbie like he expected him to loot the place.

...

I wondered about the threshold between sober and drunk. I had a glass of rosé most evenings as I stood in the window watching the light dissipate. I watched the subtle shifts of colour in the scene before me, the earth skating toward autumn giving Montréal a golden glow. I longed for the brilliant fire of leaves, which were starting to show their age.

Some nights this intoxicated me, others it didn't. Some nights I refilled the glass, others I didn't.

...

Two days before classes started, I sat in the park beside the Visual Arts building with a coffee and pretended to smoke a cigarette, taking dramatic drags off my Du Maurier and blowing the smoke out without inhaling.

I watched people walking past in their fall outfits: trench coats, chinos, little leather bags. It wasn't that I was particularly interested in fashion, but in these material forms of self-expression. Each ensemble felt like a little window of possibility into the kind of person I could become.

A few wore berets. I was desperate for a beret. I crossed my arms over my dull grey sweater and pulled out my phone.

...

The day before classes started, I bought a beret.

Black. Classic. I wore it around the apartment, passing by mirrors and trying to catch myself in them. There was something so dissatisfying about buying something frivolous that for a moment had seemed a kind of solution.

...

I didn't consider myself particularly affected by my father. It was Mother I answered to. He was never violent, not really. Just uninterested.

...

Uncle Robbie was babysitting or we were spending the day together or at least I don't remember Mother being there. And he was pulling up YouTube videos of his favourite music, dancing across the rug in the living room, turning it up loud. He danced like a teenager. I maybe thought of him as a teenager.

He hauled me up off the couch and said something like, Feel the music or Let the music set you free, or maybe he was just singing along.

I remember adoring him in that moment, like a cool older brother who could show me a world beyond my parents'.

I asked for the same song three times in a row and he promised to take me to a concert that summer.

Then Mother came home and told him to stop and I felt like I'd been peering in a window to someone else's life, and the blinds suddenly flipped closed.

...

My phone died several days ago. I watched the green in the battery icon ooze slowly out, away, into blank space until just one drop remained. Turned red. Then that too was gone. I watched this death with fascination. I could be truly alone. I never did unpack my phone charger.

When I opened my laptop hours later, there were four emails from Mother.

Why is your phone turned off?

Is this some kind of joke?

Levi, where on earth have you been? I have been trying to contact you. How am I supposed to know where you are? That you are okay? If you don't answer me, I will be forced to call the police and file a missing persons report.

The blue light sliced into my retinas and I snapped the computer shut. The air around my temples pounded like fists on a locked door. I poured myself a drink.

…

Chloé was giving me a look. The look she gives me when she knows something I haven't said. When she sees something I haven't shown. It was a look I knew well.

Lev, she said. Je dois l'entendre de toi. Dis-moi.

Tell you what?

She stared at me. My fingers pushed at the loose skin of my left elbow.

She said, Fuck off.

My arms were tingling in a way that made me aware of their boundaries. The heat of the afternoon sun and the city street below pressed in on my skin. Sweat squeezed from my pores.

Lev. Don't do this, she said. Je t'en prie.

Do what?

I turned toward the sliding glass door that led from the balcony back into my apartment. The glass reflected my hunched shoulders, drawn nearly to my ears. I tried to release them.

Just say it. Out loud.

Why?

I turned back. Her arms were wrapped around her body as if conserving heat, though her eyes burned.

Why did you move here, then?

I don't know, I said. I didn't know. I mean, I couldn't be completely sure.

Two short streams of air pulsed from her nostrils like a bull who's seen a red flag.

Do you even know how fucking selfish you are?

Was I stung by this? Or was it the way she narrowed her eyes like she had me cornered?

It's not like that, I said.

Bien. Then what is it like?

I—

She waited, arms crossed.

I just need some space to work things out. On my own.

The fire in Chloé's eyes burned molten and I braced for the eruption, but she just stood in one quick motion, wrenching the balcony door open, disappearing inside, slamming the front door.

I tried calling after her, but the sound I made was so small.

It wasn't what she was waiting to hear. But maybe it was what I was waiting to say.

The series of bangs all echoed off each other, surrounding me like children calling for violence on a schoolyard.

...

I retreated inside, let the dark room hold me, let my eyes adjust.

THREE

I tried not to think about Chloé. Her words began to cross my mind as if across a marquee, like Mother's so often did. They began to mix. Fragments smashed together. Which of them had said it?

You will never tell anyone / You will never be free.

...

I stood in the aisle with the hammers, staring at the range of them. I chose the only one with a wooden handle among the rubber and plastic in shades of electric yellow, felt its weight in my hand. I picked nails at random out of the different bins. Tried not to think about Chloé, how she'd know what to do.

Fine, I thought, I will learn.

Back at the apartment, I stared at the massive framed poster of my favourite painting, at the nails, then at the wall. All of this seemed insurmountable.

I didn't know which size nail to use, so I smashed three into the blank white wall, faintly aware, I'm sure, of the mess I was making.

I hung the poster and stood back to see if it was level. Immediately I was swept into the uneasy relations of the image, the people in the corner café late at night. Everyone seemed to be separate, hunched, drawn together in this small patch of light that spilled into the dark street through wide windows. As if on display.

I would say that I hadn't heard the creaking sound, but then how would I remember it?

Everything smashed to the ground, nails and all, and glass shot in every direction.

...

How do you do it? I'd slurred one night, walking behind Chloé and Melissa as we made our way back to their place from Gerts, McGill's campus bar. They were always a few steps ahead.

Chloé kept walking, but Melissa let go of her hand, turned back to me.

What do you mean? they said. Do what?

I was unsteady. Unsure what I'd asked. What I really wanted to know.

You talk to people so easily. It's just. How do you. You know. How do you connect with people like that?

I was thinking of the cute boy from trivia who had gotten the question about Edward Hopper, and then, when it was over, somehow he and Chloé and I were standing in a little circle, and Chloé kept saying something and then looking pointedly at me as though this was a play we'd rehearsed and it was my line next and then he would look at me too and then my body would change shape and they would both look away, Chloé grimacing.

I almost missed the look Melissa and Chloé exchanged then. I felt a flash of irritation—Chloé could be so belittling—but quickly a warmth, maybe even gratitude. Melissa fell into step beside me, nodded to themself.

Well, they said, I mean, I guess you just have to find something to start a conversation with.

I was about to ask, Yes, but what do I start with? when Chloé whipped around. My spine curved.

You just have to be yourself. You have to know who you are and what you want and what you stand for. Tu veux quoi, Lev?

I mumbled something dismissive, not even willing to commit to an I don't know, and carried on along behind them in silence, suddenly feeling quite sober aside from the urge to be sick.

...

I didn't get invited out much in high school. I mean, I didn't really have any friends. But out of some group-spiritedness, Emily from my art class invited me to her graduation party. I don't know what made me go. Curiosity, I suppose. I've always been more drawn to beginnings, but I guess with endings there is less to lose.

I drifted from room to room with my bottle of sauv blanc and my red plastic cup. Everyone was shouting at each other and laughing, these people I had seen every day for five years but knew nothing about.

I found myself perched on the arm of a couch on one clenched ass cheek. On the coffee table, all dark wood and glass, this guy Kevin divided up lines of powder with his Opus card and someone was saying, Man, where did you get that?

Across the room, a boy I didn't know was inspecting an objet from the shelf behind him, something turquoise and glassy. As he ran a finger across the bulbous thing in his hands, I realized my finger was mirroring his, along my plastic cup. I sat on my hand. His cheekbones were high and his eyebrows dark.

Kevin called out to me, offered me his Opus card. He had never spoken to me before. I shook my head.

When I looked up again, the guy by the shelf was looking right at me. My blood jumped. I took a gulp of wine, gagged on it.

...

On the balcony with coffee. I looked down at the street, where groups of people in twos and threes were pulled along to the metro station that connected to every university in the city. Every muscle in me was clenched. I could leave through this doorway, walk through another one. I could put myself into the scene of the morning. I could step into the fantasy playing across my mind where I put on the velvet loafers and the loose buttoned shirt, followed the path of people, walked into the Arts building. I let that fantasy take hold and I stood perfectly still, long after class had ended and I had gone nowhere.

...

I was on the back deck of the house, taking deep breaths in the shadows, when I heard the door slide open. Persistent bass music and shouting slithered out into the mist. I turned.

The boy who'd held the glass objet lit a cigarette, said, I hate parties. Offered me a smoke.

I took it, rolled it between my fingers. I'd never smoked before. This struck me as a lame thing to admit. I brought it to my lips. They seemed to hum against the paper.

He leaned in, flicked his lighter. A flame shot up and disappeared. Here, he said, cupping a hand around the lighter, his fingertips brushing the soft skin of my palm. Our eyes met above the flame. I felt his stare in the blood that rose to my cheeks. Heat spread all through me.

And then the cigarettes and the lighter were discarded and the space between our faces was closing in.

...

Silence was such a pleasure. Or rather, the sounds of solitude. The drip of a tap, low refrigerator hum, wind outside moving through space. I tuned like a radio dial into the frequency of solitude.

...

On another day I did make it out the door, I did make it to the Arts building. Every threshold was a struggle. I had spent the week longing for this beginning, and now it seemed to be rejecting me like an antigen.

I sat at the very back, let the weight of the lecture pull me under. I thought of Chloé, burning bright in a Poli Sci class at this very moment. Probably interrupting the class with one of her testy debates. I thought of my apartment. I slipped out the back door of the lecture hall, pretending I hadn't understood the prof's call.

Hé. Monsieur. Y'a un problème?

On the street outside, choked brown leaves had already begun to collect in the gutters.

...

When I woke on Chloé and Melissa's couch the morning after Gerts, my head felt thick and muddy. I lifted myself gingerly, made for the kitchen, let tap water flow into a Smash the Patriarchy mug. There was no other sound in the apartment.

I usually hung around on such mornings, waited to see if I would be included in their day. Sometimes, on weekdays like this, we would go for coffee on Saint-Laurent, exchanging memories of the night before, before stumbling to class in last night's clothes. These moments of camaraderie were so thrilling.

That morning, though, I slipped out as quietly as I could. I skirted campus and walked along Sherbrooke, found myself standing outside the Musée des Beaux-Arts. It had been my favourite place to come as a kid. Something in the hushed awe of the place, the way people would stare at the paintings, have private little interactions with them. It felt important.

I walked through the entrance hall, sliced with sparkling triangles from the glass ceiling overhead, and flipped through the brochure.

There was a new modern art exhibition. I made for the gallery. At the end of the room was a painting by Edward Hopper. I was drawn to the greenish, glassy haze of the painting. I was familiar with *Nighthawks*, but hadn't realized how it would reel me in like a fish.

The glow of light spilling onto the street through the window. The people inside distant from one another, with nowhere to be but a corner café, brightly lit as a television screen in the night. Alone but on display.

I thought of the boy from trivia, wondered whether he knew this painting. Whether he had stood in this very spot, staring at it, feeling exposed.

I stopped in the gift shop, bought the largest poster they had of the painting, carried it carefully home all the way across Sherbrooke and up Mountain Avenue. I didn't dare take the bus for fear of buckling it, though it was packaged in a long cardboard tube.

...

I deleted several more emails from Mother without reading them. Eventually just marked her as spam.

...

Sometimes I felt like a goldfish in a pet shop, only able to grow as much as my container allowed. Always coming up against the glass, turning away so I didn't have to look too closely.

...

And then he kissed me and I was reaching out for him. His tongue caressed mine, all my muscles turned to liquid. There was a noise from inside and he grabbed my hand and led me through the damp grass, out behind the garden shed. His eyes glinted in the dark and his smile reassured me as he placed his hands firmly on my hips. Something in my stomach dropped, like the sensation of airplane turbulence, and my penis grew a little tight against my jeans. He pushed me gently against the shed. I was frozen. I was melting. I wanted to launch myself at him. I wanted to reach for the hard outline in his tight jeans. I wanted to stand perfectly still and let him lead the way.

His eyes were locked on mine. He slowly unbuttoned his jeans, and his penis sprung out, head glistening. He took my hand and I nodded and he wrapped it gently around the tip. That juice sticky like peach nectar felt delicious on my hand and I began to stroke his length with it. His head tipped back, exposing his neck and sternum beneath his V-neck shirt. My skull throbbed, blood rushed to my penis, and he gave a little moan. He fumbled for my zipper and yanked my pants to my feet in one swift motion. I leaned back against the wall as he grabbed my ass and swallowed me whole. Brilliant colours flashed against the insides of my eyelids, every flick of his tongue ripping me apart, every motion of his hands gluing me back together with gold.

And then, just as he blew life into me, voices ripped through the night. Someone was shouting, Ew, what the fuck, while another voice called, Holy shit, who is it? My eyes slid in and out of focus as I shuddered against the damp shed siding, legs buckling, cum shooting up, streaking both my shirt and the boy's.

...

There was a DM from Chloé. I didn't know if I wanted to open it. Would it be an apology? Was that what I wanted?

I opened the message.

Call your mother, she's looking for you.

...

When we had cleaned up, exchanged eye contact and soft brushes of fingers on skin, the boy slipped his phone number in my pocket, along with his name, Jean-Pierre, and he went back inside first. I held my hands up in front of me, admiring the ribbons of gold glinting on my skin.

As I reached for the handle of the sliding glass door, I heard a shriek of laughter. Something inside me turned cold. I turned, walked toward the garden gate.

...

I typed *gay bars* into Google. The map showed me sitting in my fake leather chair, surrounded by places to not be alone. An actual rainbow of options encircling my location.

I looked at the photos of each bar: velvet discos, cavernous speakeasies, piano bars, cocktail bars, bars to replicate every era. I wanted to see every one of them. I shut my laptop.

...

I did wonder sometimes whether it was healthy to spend so much time in retreat. In some ways I knew that there was a limit, a threshold. But I didn't know where that was and how close I might be to it.

...

I sipped wine from the bottle as I walked home from the party, trying to reach through the misty dark for the elation I had felt not ten minutes before.

The gold crumbled, cracked, lay in dust at my feet. Something about the way it shimmered suddenly seemed off.

It would be a long time before I knew what to do with the rest of the pieces.

...

That night, up in my bedroom, I opened my phone, stared at Uncle Robbie's Montréal number. I wished I could call him, ask what to do. He was the only one who ever seemed to want to listen to what I was saying, rather than trying to reroute my words like an inconvenient river.

But Robbie had moved to Vancouver a few years back. Left without a word. Stayed gone without a word.

...

I still have Jean-Pierre's number, tucked away in a book on Japanese pottery, innocent as a bookmark. It is worn in places from the number of times I have taken it out and stared at it over the years. I never did call.

FOUR

I plugged my phone in. I watched the empty black of the screen glow a brighter shade. A red battery sign appeared. Two percent. Five. Every muscle in my face was taut as I powered it on.

Voicemails. Messages. Chloé. Mother. Chloé.

...

Until the summer I was eleven, I had a best friend named Toby who lived a few houses up the hill. Our parents let us wander between yards in the summer. I adored Toby. He was always painting his imagination across the air between us so I could see too. He came up with fantastic games in a single sentence.

The police are on the way, we have to hide the evidence.

We were in his backyard and from whatever wisp of an idea had come to him, he was already fully immersed, combing the grass and stuffing his pockets with leaves. I don't know what made me say it.

And we have to take our clothes off.

A second, a beat. It hung in the air and I tensed my legs to run away.

Then he said, Okay, but we have to climb the tree so nobody sees.

...

She showed up at the door. I was staring at Chloé's name on my phone, thumb hovering over the message notification, thinking about opening it, and then there she was with her fist and the wood of the door.

She marched in and sat down. I took my time closing the door and facing her.

I'm sorry, Lev.

She was wearing her look of combative fierceness and I think I saw then that it wasn't directed at me. It never had been. I think I saw then that she was exhausted. She was still wearing her work shirt and she smelled like coffee.

I sat down beside her and told her about that night with Jean-Pierre all those years ago and I sobbed so hard I could barely get the words out and she put her arm around me and she looked like she might cry too if that was her way of dealing with things.

...

One winter break, Uncle Robbie asked me what I wanted to be when I grew up. I didn't even look up from the picture I was drawing. I'm going to be an economist, I said automatically. I'm not sure I even knew what that meant. I'm still not sure I really do. But that's what my father did, and it's what he'd told me I was supposed to do. I kept drawing, not lifting my hand from the page, trying to make faces from the shapes I conjured.

Uncle Robbie was hovering, watching me. I could tell that his eyes were following my hand. Every now and then they would peer up at my face. I was used to this sort of thing by then. Adults studying me as though I was exhibiting strange behaviour.

After a while Robbie said, No, but Levi, what do you want to do?

It seemed to me that every one of those words was emphasized, so I had trouble picking out which one he'd stressed. It also seemed to me that nobody had ever really asked that question, with any emphases at all.

Well, I said, I like to draw. I like seeing the paintings at the gallery. Exhibitions. I like exhibitions. Is there a person that makes those? I'd like to be an exhibitionist.

Robbie's head flopped back and he laughed and I bent over my drawing to hide the heat in my face. He put a hand on my shoulder and said that's what I should be.

...

Chloé said, I have to get to the library. But come with me.

On the metro, she held my hand. I looked down, watched her thumb stroke the skin of my wrist, and her breakup with Melissa hit me. I'd hardly asked a thing about it. I had been sad myself, because I liked Melissa, but they'd been fighting toward the end.

Chloé had been quiet about it, hadn't brought it up. I let her not bring it up.

I should have known better.

I closed my eyes to hide the tears that were forming as we rode through the darkness together, flashes of light popping and rushing past.

...

In the morning before I went to Toby's, I'd taken my mother's laptop from her desk and sat cross-legged on my bed with it. I typed *penis* into the search bar. I was amazed by how easy it was. My finger on the touchpad flinched toward the *X* at the top of the page. But I had already seen. Thick, powerful dicks with veins bulging like overstuffed sausages threatening to burst through their flimsy skin. I scrolled through the photos, staring at these penises standing out from their bodies like things with a power all their own. I pulled my shorts down and looked at my own small, limp penis slumped against my leg.

...

A warm longing caught my breath when I saw the green glass lamps, the tall oak columns of my favourite reading room at McGill. The sun falling through a stained glass window left blue-and-gold pools stretched across the parquet. Chloé slid into a chair and arranged her books around her. I was slow to settle, thumbing the worn leather strap of my bag.

But I guess sometimes the only way forward is through. I opened my laptop.

The blank white space of the email text box stared back at me. I typed greeting after greeting, testing tones. Hello Mother. Hi Mom. Dear Brigid. I erased them all. Decided to skip this step.

Do you have a phone number or email for Robbie?

I hit Send. Slipped out of the fluorescent library into the warm bath of the afternoon.

...

Toby and I scurried up the limbs of a maple with its dense cover of soft new leaves. I could have kissed the bursting buds. I hadn't seen another boy naked before. The images of thick, veiny penises from that morning felt so distant from this moment.

We took turns removing articles of clothing, hanging them delicately over the branches above until we were surrounded as much by leaves as by a clothesline. This extra veil between us and the world below where Toby's parents were sipping lemonade somewhere felt like it created a space all our own.

We stared at each other. Toby's penis was wider than mine, and there were a few dark hairs sprouting around it. I didn't have any hairs.

Toby was ready. Okay, he said, pretend you're an alien and you have to inspect me to see if I am an alien or a human.

I reached out, glad to be following his lead. I felt the bristly texture of the curly hairs. I glanced up at his face, seeking a reaction. There was none.

Keep going, he said. You have to make a thorough report to the director.

I trailed my trembling fingers down to his penis, wrapping it in my hand. I was breathing hard. It felt like those energy drinks that were banned at school were swirling around inside me.

I shifted closer to him, suddenly wanting to make his penis hard and veiny like the photos, to stand up from his body. He spread his legs a little farther apart.

Toby's balance shifted. He tumbled backward, smashing through the leaves and branches on the way down.

...

A few weeks after that winter break, I turned twelve. It was the first birthday party that Uncle Robbie came to. It was the adult kind of birthday party where there was dinner and cake and we all wore our nice clothes. And by we all, I mean Mother, Uncle Robbie, and me. My father hadn't remembered my birthday in years, and I hadn't heard from him at all since he'd left that summer.

Mother was wearing a stiff dress the colour of sand. Robbie had a tie with little flowers on it.

Then he handed me a present wrapped in gold, and inside there was a heavy book on contemporary painting with glossy photographs, and a watercolour paint kit.

I sobbed like a busted fire hydrant.

...

For once, my mother didn't respond to an email.

I opened a new tab in my browser. Typed his name in the search bar.

A white screen. Links like bullet points. A Twitter account. A LinkedIn profile. A headline: MONTREAL QUEER CULTURE PUBLICATION WELCOMES LONG-TIME CONTRIBUTOR ROBBIE MALONE AS NEW EXECUTIVE DIRECTOR. Beside this a small, square photo. A face I knew well. But with new lines.

Ad Hommeinem. A magazine Chloé was always reading.

I clicked the headline. Stared at the fifty-word bio of what his life now contained. He played the trumpet. Enjoyed cooking, travel, and jazz music. He had a cat.

A Google search. That's all it had taken to find him.

...

Toby had yelled, and I scrambled down to see his elbow bent at an absurd angle, one I couldn't comprehend at first, and he was screaming and his mother was running toward us, then slowing as her eyes tripped on the sight. She was staring not at Toby's elbow, I realized, but at our naked bodies.

She yelled for her husband to call an ambulance. She was running back toward the house as she turned and banished me from the yard. I looked back at Toby, still sprawled and screeching under the tree.

...

My father was in the front room when I got home, and our eyes met through the window as I walked up the driveway. I saw a look of repulsion cross his face. I had left my clothes in the tree.

When I opened the door, I thought he might hit me. But instead, he lifted the gaze off me, turned, and laid it upon my mother, who withered and began to sob. He shook his head and walked away. Mother looked up at me through the tears, then turned away too.

It was some time before I realized that this was the last time I saw my father.

FIVE

I thought about asking Chloé. She would want to march straight to Mother's and demand the truth about Uncle Robbie. But I had a feeling this was something I needed to do on my own.

It was a bold feeling, a sense of certainty. I knew on some level that asking Mother wouldn't accomplish anything. Neither Chloé nor I could ask her for the truth and still trust that she didn't believe, on some level, that she was telling it.

Is there even such a thing as truth when it comes to the past, or is there only memory?

...

I poured a drink.

I put Hall and Oates on my phone, stuck the speaker into the martini shaker. The echo was horrible and tinny and I loved it.

I poured a drink.

I tried my loafers on.

I poured a drink.

I danced to "You Make My Dreams" in front of the mirror. I spilled wine on the rug.

I poured a drink.

I opened up the Google search for gay bars on the block.

I poured a drink.

I stumbled out the door and nearly left my keys in the lock. I headed for a bar called Jukebox that had the coolest photo online. Old records plastered all over the walls.

I ordered a drink.

...

I opened my laptop and read his bio on the *Ad Hom-meinem* website again. The trumpet, the cat, the jazz. The words Robbie had arranged into a neat paragraph to tell the internet who he was. The space between us ripping open like an ocean. How long had it been since I'd last seen him, ten years?

The walls of my apartment seemed hazy, insubstantial. What was my relation to this space, to this flimsy life I had built? To the one I had left? Were they really so different?

I opened the next link, his Facebook. The little message icon. I hovered my cursor over it. Felt the blood gasping through my chest, unsure whether it was my heart beating louder or the silence around me that magnified it. I clicked. There he was, at the other end of this blank message box. My fingers spread over the assortment of letters that could make up some kind of plea.

And what plea? He'd been here in Montréal all this time. He was the one who had disappeared.

...

I sat by the bar at Jukebox, tucked in the corner, watching. I thought about where I was and I wanted to send a picture to Chloé and I nearly did but something stopped me.

I ordered a drink.

I became aware that someone had sat down on the next stool.

I love this song, he said, nodding toward the jukebox. I'm Sanka.

Lev. I don't know this one, I said. Thick bass notes hung in the air.

I ordered a drink.

I tried to think of what to say. I didn't know what to say.

Come dance with me, Sanka said.

...

The day before, I'd put on a nice shirt and jacket and I walked the four blocks down Sainte-Catherine, emotions gurgling in my stomach and making a run for it up my esophagus.

When I hit the sidewalk, I had been pointed toward UQAM, filled with resolve. I'd only been to one lecture since term began two weeks ago. But as I looked up and saw the rainbow installation stretching above me like some kind of protective layer, I turned the other direction.

The *Ad Hommeinem* offices were above a corner café in a brick building that was so narrow I wondered how furniture could have been navigated into the space. Through the plain glass door. Up stairs with rubber treads on the edges that held my feet steady as I climbed. I kept telling myself this hallway could be any hallway, could lead to any space.

The office was small and bright. *Ad Hommeinem* was painted on the wall in big yellow letters. Half a dozen mismatched desks were scattered around the room, near the windows, piled with books and papers. Busy-looking people.

The scene before me carried on like a play. I wondered if I could pass back through the door and down the stairs without disturbing this balance.

Are you here for an interview? A tall person in a vivid-green blazer was coming toward me, clutching a stack of old notebooks.

A few others started to turn my way. I searched their faces over the person's shoulder, until I saw him, there at the back of the room. He was balancing his phone between his ear and shoulder, a coffee mug in one hand. He looked up.

Robbie looked older than I expected, his dark mane mostly silver now, and cropped closer to his head. His eyes had sunken into his face a little, and now they were wide and round as he let the phone fall from his shoulder.

Robbie, I whispered. Out of the corner of my eye I was aware that the attention of the room had shifted, the others looking back and forth between us. Robbie's body seemed rigid. The kind of slowness that comes from conflicting neural messages. Every instant of his hesitation seemed to push me closer to the door.

Has something happened? Is your mother okay?

...

At Jukebox, I let Sanka take my hand, lead me toward the crowd, the music, the people. Heat from his hand shot up my arm in waves, and I stared into the dark, dense mass of his curls. I watched the way his hips swayed as he walked. I watched his hand holding mine.

He led me to the jukebox. He said, Put on something funky. Something we can groove to.

I slid a toonie in and I stood there in front of the machine feeling the heft of this moment, this choice bearing down upon me, but the liquor and the heat seemed to surge up to meet it and they swirled above me. I pressed a finger on Hall and Oates.

He gave a laugh, the beautiful trill of a spring sparrow, and he conjured my body to his in a way that left me feeling weightless, lifted.

Old school, he murmured. I dig it.

I let Sanka lead me, unsure whether my own feet could carry me through. Then he broke away and spun himself around, arms up, and ground his hips like a sexier Patrick Swayze and I saw vivid turquoise ribbons of self twirling around him. I stood there a moment wondering what colour my ribbons would be.

He tried to gather me into him again, but I held back. I wanted ribbons. I closed my eyes and listened to the song. Really listened. Transcribed the rhythm into my body, the body that was mine. I was trying to dance in my own mind. Suddenly this concept was too much and a laugh tumbled from my throat like speech.

I let thought drift from me like smoke as I opened my eyes, hips moving. Dancing the way I had in my bedroom. He spun in circles around me until we were back in each other's arms, singing:

Oo-oo! Oo! Oo!

And then his lips. In the middle of the crowded dance floor, just his lips and mine moving so slowly the song seemed to be moving in half time or less, the voices distorted.

But there was no sound, no people. The only senses engaged were in my lips. And the electricity setting off sparks all over my body. My fingers were tracing the tendons between his ear and shoulder. He had one strong hand on my back, the other was in my hair.

He kissed me harder. The music, the crowd all sped back up as I held him more frantically. He came up for air.

Lev, babe. How new are you to the area? He looked at me with sudden seriousness.

I nodded. New, I said. My heart was taking up all the space in my chest. Still, I held his gaze.

Let's just dance, he said. I looked at him. And maybe you could give me your number, he added.

...

When he hugged me, Robbie said, I'm sorry that was my first reaction. I guess that's where your mind goes when you get old.

I held my body stiff at first, but when he didn't let go, I hid my eyes in his shoulder and wept.

...

In the hardware store, I giggled at the words *stud finder*. A guy passing by leaned in and said, More accurate than Grindr, I think we can all agree, and the warmth of mutual understanding filled me long after the instant had passed and he had moved on.

...

What colour were my ribbons? I asked Sanka at the bar, ordering another drink. He laughed. Motioned to the bartender to cancel the order.

I let him hail me a cab. I even got in before I remembered I lived on the next block.

...

Robbie said, So tell me, do you still draw?

He'd taken me to a little café I had never noticed before, in an alley in the Vieux-Port. The walls were crammed full of early modern paintings in gilded frames and the light was low. He was sipping a glass of wine, reaching for another olive from a dish the server had laid out when we sat down.

I don't know if I was surprised by this question — after all, it had been my passion the last time we'd seen each other — but something about it shook me. As though I'd forgotten some kind of promise.

Not really, I said, speaking for the first time since the office. I pressed my fingernails deep into the fleshy pad of my left thumb to distract myself from the pressure that was building up in my esophagus with all the words I had thought I wanted to say but which now seemed too sharp and angular.

Robbie showed no signs of disappointment. If anything, he looked embarrassed.

I always wondered, he said, but I guess they didn't encourage you. He let out a sigh, a long and tired sound. She wasn't always like this, you know. She stuck up for me when I came out. She was only fifteen when she came to live with me and Ben.

I fidgeted. I hadn't known this. I can't imagine my mother sticking up for anyone, I said. Her face was already contorting in my mind. Taking on a different shape.

I think she regretted it later, he said darkly. Once we tested positive, she didn't want us around you. He looked down at his glass. Not to mention your father. Are you in touch now?

I shook my head.

Robbie nodded, sucking on another olive. I don't know what you know, he said, but he was a fucking prick. The best thing he ever did for you was leave.

And why did you? Leave, I mean.

Robbie gave me a sad smile. I didn't want to, he said.

On the walk back to his office, he stopped to light a cigarette. I was only doing what Brigid asked. I thought if I didn't go with it, your parents might take it out on you. He gave me an appraising look. Maybe I fucked up.

...

I slid the stud finder along the wall until I hit the mark and carefully tapped the nail in. The curtain rod was easy, just a wooden dowel from the hardware store cradled in the right kind of hooks.

As it turned out, there was something satisfying in doing things properly.

The curtains themselves had been trickier. Harder to get right. I had opened the IKEA website only to slam my laptop shut. No.

I wound up at the Fripe-Prix in Hochelaga, swiping through hangers of fabrics that felt all wrong. Flimsy stained linens, dowdy mustard florals with a texture like corduroy, and bloody burgundy sets in some kind of thick, stiff satin that reminded me of Westmount.

Robbie called. He said, Come over. I have some things you might like.

In the boxes were the materials of Robbie's younger years. His old records, cracked ceramic mugs, posters from concerts in the eighties, mismatched kitchen utensils, stained paintbrushes. In a crate under a faded sheet I found paintings, mostly abstract, thick with oil.

Mine, he said, as I lifted one out to examine it. If you can believe that.

I said, I didn't know you were a painter.

He smiled, passed me a Fauvist-style portrait, all bold lines, yellows and blues, a young man stretched out on a long red chair. On the matting was the name "Ben Lévesque, 1964–1992." I used to be, he said.

Ben, I said.

Robbie turned away. Your generation, he said. Lost so many queer elders. Those of us left were too traumatized to be there for you. Or we were pushed out of your lives completely.

Would you mind if I borrowed these? I said.

Robbie waved a hand. Have them. I owe you that much.

I hung every painting, covered my walls with the brave strokes of them.

...

Sanka sent me a text.

Morning sunshine, how are you feeling?

...

The email had come back that morning, quicker than I'd expected. Robbie had known just who to ask at the artist-run gallery in the neighbourhood. Mr. Adler, they said. We'd be thrilled. An exhibition featuring the work of HIV-positive Montréal artists. Are you available to meet with our curator?

Mr. Adler. A name I had only ever heard my father called. I opened another tab, considered the cost of changing my last name.

...

I threaded the wooden dowel through my uncle's purple linen curtains and hung them over the patio doors where I'd stood so many nights, watching the world outside as though I wasn't a part of it.

I shut the curtains, poured a glass of wine, called Sanka.

Acknowledgements

Thanks to Karen Connelly and Lisa Moore for your mentorship.

Thanks to Lori Beck, Aaron Powell, AP Bergmann, Doug Walbourne-Gough, Cole Hayley, Nate Little, Jack Daly, and Tommy Duggan for your conversations and suggestions.

Thanks to my former agent Stephanie Sinclair, to my editor Bethany Gibson, and to the folks at Goose Lane Editions.

Chapter two of "Saint-Laurent" appeared in an early form in *Soliloquies Anthology* 23.2. Thank you for giving my work a space.

This project was funded by the Canada Council for the Arts, the Writers' Union of Canada Artist Relief Fund, ArtsNL, and the City of St. John's. Thank you.

Heather Nolan (they/them) is a novelist, poet, musician, knitwear designer, and photographer from Ktaqmkuk (Newfoundland). They are the author of *How to Be Alone*; the novella *This is Agatha Falling*, a finalist for the ReLit Award and longlisted for the BMO Winterset award; and the poetry collection *Land of the Rock: Talamh an Carraig*. Nolan's poetry and prose have been published in journals and anthologies across Canada, the US, and the UK.